W9-AFJ-362

Search-and-Rescue Dogs

BY KARA L. LAUGHLIN

The Child's World®

Published by The Child's World®
1980 Lookout Drive • Mankato, MN 56003-1705
800-599-READ • www.childsworld.com

ACKNOWLEDGMENTS
The Child's World®: Mary Berendes, Publishing Director
The Design Lab: Design
Jody Jensen Shaffer: Editing
Pamela J. Mitsakos: Photo Research

PHOTO CREDITS
© Amidala76/Dreamstime.com: 14; Andrew Burgess: leash;
AP Photo/Gregory Bull: 18; AP Photo/Krista Kennell/Sipa
Press: 21; deepspacedave/Shutterstock.com: 4; Eldadcarin/
Dreamstime.com: 9; fotostory/Shutterstock.com: cover, 1;
Jim Parkin/Shutterstock.com: 7; Lsantilli/Dreamstime.com:
11; remik44992: bone; sengulmurat/iStock.com: 17; Vasilis
Ververidis/Dreamstime.com: 12

ISBN 9781626873117
LCCN 2014934482

Printed in the United States of America
Mankato, MN
July, 2014
PA02219

ABOUT THE AUTHOR

Kara L. Laughlin is the author of eleven books for kids. She lives in Virginia with her husband and three children. They don't have a dog...yet!

TABLE OF CONTENTS

Dogs to the Rescue!

What if you had a magic nose that could smell things from far away? Would you use it to find lost people?

Some dogs do. Dogs' noses smell up to 10 million times better than people's! Dogs that find lost people are search-and-rescue (SAR) dogs. Some people get lost on hikes. Others are lost after bombings or earthquakes. SAR dogs work to save those people.

Some SAR dogs are trained to find people buried in avalanches.

Dogs have been saving lost people for a very long time. Three hundred years ago, a group of monks lived in snowy mountains. Their dogs could find people trapped in the snow.

The place where the dogs lived was called St. Bernard's Pass. The dogs became known as St. Bernards. They saved people at St. Bernard's Pass for two hundred years. They saved more than two thousand people.

Dogs were used in many wars, too. Dogs helped doctors find hurt soldiers in the first World War. In World War II, many bombs were dropped on cities. Dogs found people trapped in the **rubble**.

Today, there are about 260 SAR dogs in the United States. More than eighty countries have SAR teams. After a disaster, SAR teams go to help. Sometimes they come from all over the world.

INTERESTING FACT

Here are some places where SAR dogs have worked:

1995 Oklahoma City Bombing
2001 New York and Washington, DC; 9/11 Attacks
2005 New Orleans, LA; Hurricane Katrina
2010 Port-au-Prince, Haiti; Earthquake
2011 Tohoku, Japan; Great East Japan Earthquake

What Do SAR Dogs Do?

When people move, tiny bits of skin and hair fall away from them. Some bits fall to the ground. Some bits float on the air. Dogs can smell these tiny bits. They use them to find people.

There are three different types of SAR dogs: air scent dogs, tracking dogs, and trailing dogs. Air scent dogs smell the bits in the air. Tracking dogs use scent trails on the ground. Trailing dogs are special. They are called **scent discriminating** dogs. That means they can search for one person's special scent. They might use the air or the ground to do this.

Even though the work SAR dogs do is very serious, the dogs don't know that. They are just sniffing their way through a game of hide and seek.

This SAR dog is searching the desert for a lost person.

What Makes a Good SAR Dog?

Most SAR dogs are rescued from shelters. Some come from breeders. The best dogs for search-and-rescue teams are not always the best pets. They have a lot of energy. They like to chew and dig. They also take big risks. That's great for search-and-rescue, but not always great in a home.

SAR dogs need to have a strong "toy drive." That means they like to grab at things and tug. They also need a strong "hunt drive." That means they will try to find a toy no matter what. They also need to be very brave.

Many dogs with these traits are herding and sporting dogs. Labrador retrievers, German shepherds, border collies, and golden retrievers all make good SAR dogs.

Border collies like this one make excellent SAR dogs.

Training a SAR Dog

It takes years to train a SAR dog and his partner. The dogs and their partners, or **handlers**, learn to work as a team. They learn voice commands and hand motions that tell the dog what to do. The handler has to know her dog very well. She is asking the dog to do a dangerous job. It's her job to keep the dog safe.

INTERESTING FACT
Disaster sites are dangerous places. There is broken glass and metal. SAR dogs learn a special "soft walk" to keep their paws from being hurt.

These dogs and their handlers are at a training exercise.

Training starts with basic **obedience**. Dogs learn to sit, stay, and lie down. They also practice bravery: they walk on wobbly floors. They go into tunnels. (Most dogs hate tunnels!) These skills are needed in the places where they search.

The Nose Knows

Trainers teach SAR dogs to follow their noses. To do this, a trainer hides a toy. Then he will set up challenges to make it hard to find the toy. He makes loud noises. He hides food nearby. The dog must learn to find the toy no matter what. No going after food. No checking out noises. His job is just to sniff out the toy.

This SAR dog is training in rubble like it would find after an earthquake.

When a dog can find a toy, he learns to find people. A helper hides with a toy. When the dog finds the helper, the helper gives the toy to the dog. Then the helper plays with the dog. The dog learns that if he finds the toy, he gets to play.

When the handler thinks his team is ready, the team takes a test. SAR teams can get Advanced (Type 1) or Basic (Type 2) Certification. Type 2 means the dog can find people with a handler close by. Type 1 means the dog can find people away from his handler. The Type 1 test is very hard. Many good search dogs never become Type 1 SAR dogs.

INTERESTING FACT

Dogs can be different. Some dogs don't care about playing after they find their toy. Their handlers give them other rewards.

This SAR dog is signaling that it has found something.

The Life of a SAR Dog

Most of the time, a SAR team's job is just staying ready. Dogs might go months or years between jobs. Practice keeps the team ready. SAR teams practice searching once or twice a week.

Every SAR job is different, so SAR teams practice in many types of places. Then they are ready for many types of jobs.

SAR dogs often work after disasters. A lot of the time, the handler can't go with the dog onto the site. The handler uses hand signals to direct the dog. When a dog finds a person, he will whine and scratch. He won't leave the spot. The handler tells the rest of his team that the dog has found someone. Then the team figures out how to get to the person.

INTERESTING FACT
More than 300 search-and-rescue dogs helped out at Ground Zero in the hours and days after the 9/11 attacks in 2001.

A Hard Day
At Work

Sometimes when SAR teams come, they don't find survivors. This can be hard for the dog and the handler. The want to find people alive!

Some dogs are trained to find people who were killed. This is called **recovery**. People say that knowing what happened to the people they loved makes it easier to say goodbye. They are grateful for the work these dogs do.

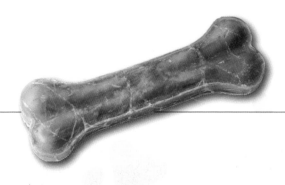

This SAR team is working together
after an earthquake in Turkey.

Hunter, the Search-and-Rescue Hero

After the earthquake in Haiti, Mr. Monahan and Hunter had to search in dangerous rubble like this.

In 2010, an earthquake hit Port-au-Prince, Haiti. Buildings had collapsed. Many people died. Some people were trapped under rubble. SAR Teams from all over the world went to Haiti to help. One team was from Ojai, California. Bill Monahan and his border collie, Hunter, were on that team.

Hunter's team was one of the first to arrive. Hunter started searching. He searched for hours. Hunter didn't find anyone.

On the second day of their search, Hunter started whining and scratching near a building that had collapsed. Mr. Monahan showed the other people on his team where Hunter had found people. Later that day, three teenaged girls were rescued from the rubble of the building. When they got out, people cheered.

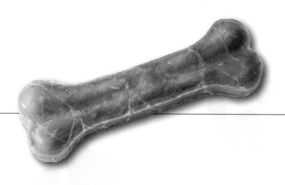

Hunter's team rescued twelve people in Haiti. When they returned to California, they were heroes.

Today, Hunter is still working with Mr. Monahan. Mr. Monahan says this about Hunter: "I think he will go beyond just being a good search dog and will be one of the great ones!"

INTERESTING FACT
More than 175 dogs helped to search for survivors after the earthquake in Haiti. Together, they found more than 70 survivors.

Hunter and Bill Monahan are a great search-and-rescue team!

handlers (HAND-lerz) People who work with SAR dogs. Their dogs are their partners.

obedience (oh-BEE-dee-enss) When a dog can be counted on to do what he is told to do.

recovery (ree-KOV-er-ee) The act of finding human remains.

rubble (RUB-bul) Piles of brick, wood, glass, and metal that used to be buildings.

scent discriminating (SENT dis-KRIM-ih-nay-ting) Scent discriminating dogs can follow a person's scent trail to that exact person.

IN THE LIBRARY

Bozzo, Linda. *Search and Rescue Dog Heroes*. Berkeley
Heights, NJ: Bailey Books/Enslow. 2011.

Engle, Margarita. *When You Wander: A Search and
Rescue Dog Story.* New York: Henry Holt. 2013.

ON THE WEB

Visit our Web site for links about search-and-rescue dogs:
www.childsworld.com/links

*Note to Parents, Teachers, and Librarians: We routinely check our Web links to
make sure they're safe, active sites—so encourage your readers to check them out!*

INDEX